MARC BROWN

ARTHUR'S THANKSGIVING

Little, Brown and Company

BOSTON   TORONTO   LONDON

For Melanie Kroupa, who,
as far as I know,
has never been a turkey

Library of Congress Cataloging in Publication Data

Brown, Marc Tolon.
  Arthur's Thanksgiving.

  Summary: Arthur finds his role as director of the
Thanksgiving play a difficult one, especially since
no one will agree to play the turkey.
  [1. Thanksgiving Day — Fiction. 2. Plays — Fiction.
3. School stories. 4. Animals — Fictions] I. Title.
PZ7.B81618Art 1983   [E]   83–798
ISBN 0-316-11060-4 (hc)
ISBN 0-316-11232-1 (pb)

HC: 10 9 8 7 6
PB: 10 9 8

WOR

JOY STREET BOOKS ARE PUBLISHED BY LITTLE, BROWN AND COMPANY (INC.)

Published simultaneously in Canada
by Little, Brown & Company (Canada) Limited

PRINTED IN THE UNITED STATES OF AMERICA

Arthur's class was so quiet, you could hear
a pin drop.
Mr. Ratburn was about to announce the director for
the Thanksgiving play, *The Big Turkey Hunt.*
Arthur chewed his pencil.
"I hope he picks me," whispered Francine.
They all held their breath.

"I've chosen Arthur to direct the play,"
said Mr. Ratburn.
He handed Arthur the script.

"Me? The director?" said Arthur.
"Oh, no," grumbled Francine.
"This is going to be a disaster."

Arthur's first job as director was to assign parts.
The narrator would have the most to say,
but the turkey, the symbol of Thanksgiving,
had the most important role of all.
Secretly, Arthur was glad he wouldn't
have to be the turkey.
But who would play that part?

At lunch, Francine gave Arthur two chocolate
cupcakes. She wanted to be the narrator.
Buster even let Arthur borrow his
Captain Zoom spaceman. He wanted to be
Governor William Bradford.
Being the director seemed like fun.

Arthur thought Francine
would make a good turkey.
"Never!" said Francine.
"I want to be the narrator.
Besides, I have the
loudest voice."
No doubt about that.
Francine would be the narrator.

Arthur showed Muffy a drawing
of the turkey costume.
"Lots of feathers," said Arthur.
"It's a very glamorous role."
"Yuk! Vomitrocious!"
squealed Muffy.
"I should be the Indian princess.
I have real braids."

"Brain, I've saved the most
intelligent part for you,"
explained Arthur.
"No way will I be the
turkey," answered the Brain.
"I'll be the Indian chief."

"Buster, you're my
best friend," began Arthur.
"The part is real easy.
Only one line, and it's the
best in the play."
"I want to be Governor Bradford,"
said Buster.

Arthur was so desperate that
he asked Binky Barnes.
"The turkey is a strong and
powerful animal," argued Arthur.
"Yeah, without saying a word,
it can make you look like a fool
in front of the entire school,"
said Binky.
The play was only six days
away. Where would Arthur
find a turkey?

Arthur knew he could count on his family.
"I'd love to be the turkey," said his father.
"But I have a dentist appointment that
I don't want to miss."

"The world is full of turkeys," joked his mother.
"You should be able to find *one*."

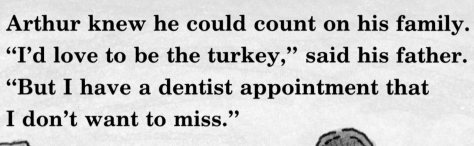

"I wouldn't be caught dead in that outfit!"
said his sister, D.W.

"Let's talk turkey," said Arthur over the PA system at school. "The best part in the Thanksgiving play is still open. If you're interested, please come to the office at once." No one came to the office.

In fact, the principal left the office, laughing. Arthur put posters in the cafeteria. He placed ads in the school paper. Nothing worked.

Arthur had other problems, too.
Muffy complained about everything.
"I should be narrator; my parents are
paying for the cast party!" she whined.
Francine would not take off her movie-star glasses.

"They're good luck," she explained, but she
was having a hard time seeing what she was doing.
Buster couldn't remember his lines.
"In 1620," he recited, "we sailed
to America on the cauliflower."

The rehearsals went from bad to worse.
"When the Pilgrims and Indians decided
to celebrate their friendship," said Francine,
"they began to hunt for a turkey."
"We cooked beans and pumpkin pies,"
whispered Sue Ellen.
"And the Pilgrim men went off to hunt for a turkey."
"We made corn bread and picked cranberries,"
said Muffy. "Oops! And the Indian braves went
on their own turkey hunt."

Then it was time for Francine to present the turkey.
"When the Indians and Pilgrims finally found
a turkey," she began, "there was great rejoicing.
Today when we think of Thanksgiving,
we think of *turkey*."
She glared at Arthur.
"Don't worry," Arthur promised.
"I told you I'd find a turkey in time."

As a last resort Arthur decided to rent a turkey.
But that wasn't such a good idea.

"If you don't get a turkey by tomorrow's performance," said Francine, "I quit."
Everyone agreed.
No turkey—no play.

Arthur went home to think.
He thought about turkeys while
he did arithmetic.

He thought about turkeys while he played the piano.

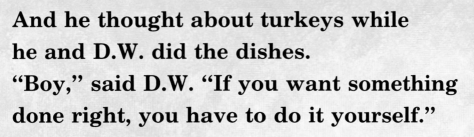

And he thought about turkeys while
he and D.W. did the dishes.
"Boy," said D.W. "If you want something
done right, you have to do it yourself."

The next morning, Francine, Muffy, and Buster stood before Arthur. They weren't taking any chances. "Do we have a turkey?" they asked. Arthur just smiled.

The whole school filed into the auditorium.
"OOOoo!" said the kids when the lights went out.
"Shhhh!" said the teachers as the curtain went up.

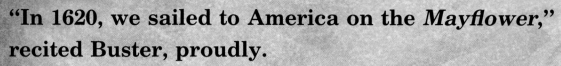

"In 1620, we sailed to America on the *Mayflower*,"
recited Buster, proudly.
"Phew!" said Arthur.
The play continued smoothly.
Muffy didn't drop the cranberries.

The Brain had his costume on correctly.
Sue Ellen said her lines in a loud, clear voice.
And Francine had even taken off
her movie-star glasses.
Then it came time for Francine's big speech.

She crossed her fingers and began.
"When the Indians and Pilgrims finally found
a turkey, there was great rejoicing.
Today, when we think of Thanksgiving,
we think of turkey."

There was a lot of fumbling behind the curtain.
Arthur took a deep breath.

He walked onstage.
As soon as he did, the audience began to laugh.
Arthur turned bright red.
This was going to be even worse
than he had thought it would be.
"The turkey," Arthur began,
"is a symbol, a symbol of . . . of . . ."
"Of togetherness and Thanksgiving!"
said a chorus of voices behind him.

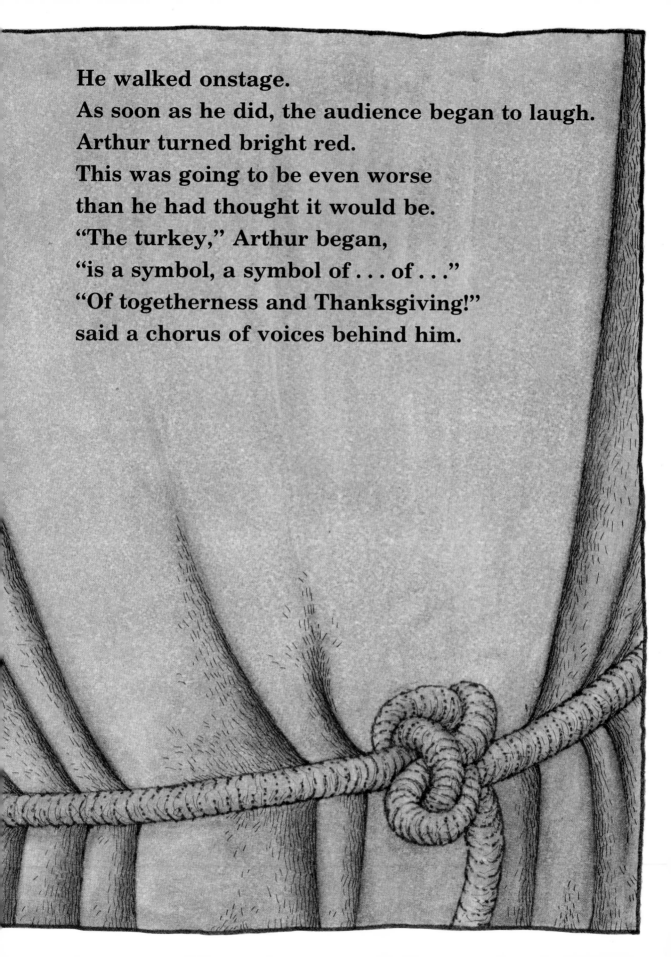

Arthur turned around and smiled.

"I guess Mom was right. The world *is* full of turkeys! Okay, turkeys, all together now. Let's hear that last line, loud and clear."